MW00777988

2021

Gemma,

No matter where you go in this big world, you'll always be my "Little Cajun Girl" May you always "be happy with yourself - that is the key!"

Happy Birthday!

Love,
Aunt Lucie & Uncle Bryan

Dedicated to:

Emilee, Ella, and Tracker

May you always have the courage
to follow your dreams.

Aileen the gator loves to dance!
She loves to sing!
She loves to prance!
She jumps and frolics,
spins and twirls!
She's a giddy gator girl.

Aileen dances each and every day,
making brand new friends along the way.
Together, dancing wherever they go,
two-step, waltz, and Zydeco!

The vast Atchafalaya,
that swamp is her maison!
It's where she makes her gumbo—
Mmmm-mmm, mais ca c'est bon!

Now you know all about Aileen,
The Cajun Dancing Gator Queen!
So come along and listen in,
the time's now for her story to begin.

One day, while swimming in her swamp,
Aileen came along ole Monsieur Chomp.
He was a rather mean and nasty fellow,
who never smiled or even said hello.

"Bonjour, Monsieur!" Aileen did say.
But Chomp just snarled and swam away.
Aileen wondered,

Mais, what is it that has him down?
Why does he always wear a frown?

She was sure of it then, that day was the day,
declaring, "I'll find out why he acts this way!"

Gliding through the basin,

swimming fast to catch up,

she looked everywhere for Chomp,

but Aileen had no luck.

She questioned the herons, the ducks, and the squirrels,
but no one could help that sweet gator girl.
Right when Aileen was ready to give up,
she heard loud, sad sniffles from the back of a stump...

"Mais what is it that has you sad?
It must be terrible! It must be bad!
Please tell me now, so I can help!
We can put you back to your normal self!"

Monsieur Chomp ashamedly hung his head,
and began to wipe the tears that had been shed.

"Promise me you will not laugh...
It's my tail—I'm missing half!
It once was long, as long could be,
until I got caught underneath a tree."

"I was stuck, and to no avail,
I tried, but could not dislodge my tail!
I yanked and tugged and pulled and shoved,
then finally was freed from all that mud."

"But when I looked back, to my despair,
only half of my tail was there!"

"Without my tail swinging to and fro,
I can't go to the fais do-do!
I'm so clumsy!
My legs aren't long!
I can't Cajun dance to a single song!
I want to dance so bad, Aileen
but how can I with no tail to swing?"

"My legs aren't steady, my knees only wobble!
I try hard to dance, but over I topple!
Tell me, Aileen, what should I do?
Oh, how I wish I was just like you!"

Aileen considered what to say,
just wanting Chomp to be okay.

"I've got a plan!" her gator eyes sparkled.
"Meet here, same spot, same time, tomorrow!"

Aileen searched all throughout the land,
and returned the next day with the Basin Band.
They played the accordion, washboard, and fiddle,
the triangle and spoons, with Aileen in the middle!

Enchanting Chomp with what she found. From his face disappeared that frown.
Many creatures, some big, some small; some petite, and still some tall.
Scales and snouts with crooked beaks, claws and fins with two left feet.
Unique colors were displayed, like a New Orleans Mardi Gras parade!

Aileen belted out a pretty melody,
and Chomp began to smile with glee.
His body, twirling round and round,
was matching movements with the sound!

"ALLONS DANSER!" Aileen shouted out.
"You're dancing, Chomp, without a doubt!"
Monsieur Chomp's moves were so sublime,
"Yes! Now I'll be dancing all the time!"
The entire basin gathered 'round to see
the duo Cajun dancing, dancing with glee.

Chomp told his friends about sweet Aileen,
and how she's the Dancing Gator Queen.
"Aileen, thanks for helping!" the creatures all cheered,
with their pal, Monsieur Chomp, now in the clear.

They ran all around and they jumped and they moved,
creating their own kind of Cajun swamp groove.
The group freely danced to the sound of the tune,
until the sun eventually gave way to the moon.

Elated, Chomp yelped, "Mais look! There we go! We made our own special fais do-do!
Merci beaucoup, mon amie, Aileen! I truly am sorry for being so mean.
I've learned so much from you today,
Aileen, ma 'tite fille, ma chère bébé !"

Chomp hugged Aileen with all of his might.
They exchanged their farewells, and bid good night.
"Bonsoir, mon ami!" the two did say

'Til next time,
laissez les bon temps rouler!

Color in Aileen, Monsieur Chomp, and all their friends!

Lightning Source UK Ltd.
Milton Keynes UK
UKRC010740101220
374765UK00002B/20